BATTING A THOUSAND

Sports Books from Thomas Nelson

If you enjoyed this book, ask your bookseller for these other fine sports titles from Thomas Nelson:

Reaching for the Rim by Bill Alexson with Terry Hill (Profiles of NBA stars. A "SportsWitness" book.)

More Than Winning by Tom Osborne with John E. Roberts

Meadowlark by Meadowlark Lemon with Jerry Jenkins

BATTING A THOUSAND

by Terry Hill

THOMAS NELSON PUBLISHERS

Nashville • Camden • Kansas City

Published in Nashville, Tennessee, by Thomas Nelson, Inc., and distributed in Canada by Lawson Falle, Ltd., Cambridge, Ontario.

Printed in the United States of America.

Scripture quotations are from the NEW KING JAMES VERSION of the Bible. Copyright © 1979, 1980, 1982, Thomas Nelson, Inc., Publisher.

library of Congress Cataloging-in-Publication Data

Hill, Terry.
  Batting a thousand.

  Summary: Provides inspirational biographical profiles
of nineteen young baseball players, who recount their
experiences as Christian sports stars.
  1. Baseball players—United States—Biography—
Juvenile literature. 2. Baseball—Religious aspects—
Christianity—Juvenile literature. [1. Baseball
players. 2. Christian life] I. Title.
GV865.A1H49   1987   796.357'092'2 [B] [920]   87-1638
ISBN 0-8407-7759-0

    3 4 5 6—92 91 90 89 88

This book is dedicated
to all those men who give so freely
of themselves to be chaplains
to major and minor league baseball teams.
The impact they have had
on men's lives
will never be fully known
in this life.

Contents

Acknowledgments

Of all the people who helped to bring this book about, I wish first of all to thank my parents, Bob and Georgia Hill. They have always encouraged me to do what is right.

Then there is my beautiful and loving wife, Dianne, who typed, transcribed, and proofed the stories in this book. Without her patience and my children's tolerance of not being with their dad many nights, this book could not have been.

I also wish to thank Marv Williams for his baseball expertise and travel with me during spring training and for teaching me there is no such thing as "good grief."

Lastly, a big thank you to all the public relations offices of the teams represented in this book. They made a rookie author feel like a pro with all of their invaluable assistance in securing interviews with the players.

OREL HERSHISER
Los Angeles Dodgers/Pitcher

"I Got Cut From My High-School Team"

I finished 1988 as Most Valuable Player in the World Series against the Oakland Athletics, Most Valuable Player in the National League Championship Series versus the New York Mets, and with a string of 59 consecutive shutout innings in the regular season, breaking Don Drysdale's old record!

I didn't think we could win the division. I didn't think we could win the playoffs. I didn't think we could win the World Series. I'll never accept that we were the better team, but that was one of my motivating factors. I felt I had to be at my best every time I pitched.

By the time the fifth and final game of the World Series came around, the pressure was really building. I kept telling myself that I didn't want this to be the bad outing. I didn't want people saying he couldn't handle the pressure. I kept pumping myself, telling myself to take it one pitch and one batter at a time. And when I'd start to rush, I started singing old hymns to myself. There's so much pressure that it's almost a spiritual experience anyway.

© 1985 Los Angeles Dodgers, Inc.

As it turned out, we won the game 5 to 2 and the World Series, four games to one over the Athletics. And even though I'd had a 23 and 8 record during the regular season and won a game and saved another in the NL Championships, I'll never forget that last game.

But my career has not always been like that, so let me tell you how I got to where I am.

I graduated from Cherry Hill East High School in New Jersey in 1976 and was fortunate to receive a partial scholarship to play at Bowling Green University in Ohio. I didn't earn a varsity letter there until my junior year. In 1979 I was drafted by the Dodgers in the seventeenth round and was sent to their farm team in Clinton, Iowa. I was a professional baseball player, I drove a Z-28 Camaro, and I had a good life. I was doing what I had always wanted to do.

While I was in Clinton, a teammate asked me if I was a Christian. I said sure, I've been to church several times, and I was born in America. Then he asked if I had a personal relationship with Jesus, and I asked him what in the world that was. I knew Jesus was this guy at church and that was it, and then my friend told me I needed Him in my life. I had never thought I had an emptiness in my life until he said that. He gave me a Bible, and I started reading it and asking him questions. The season ended in September, and I was invited to play winter ball in Arizona. When I got there, my friend was there also, and I asked him to be my room-mate. We talked quite a bit more, and then one night in Mesa, Arizona, at the Buckaroo Hotel, I got on my knees and invited Christ into my life. There were no bangs or lightning flashes, but I knew I had a peace in my heart and the emptiness was gone.

Since I had already been reading the Bible, I knew there were things I needed to start doing. I didn't drink or smoke or do drugs, but I was very jealous of other players who were more suc-cessful than I was. And when I pitched a bad game, I would get totally frustrated. Now Christ has taught me to do my best, and when others do bet-ter, I can say, "Good for them!" and mean it. I can also thank Him for the bad times as well as the good.

People ask me how I handle the pressure of fifty thousand people watching me pitch. Well, it's easy when you know in your heart that a baseball game doesn't mean that much. Yes, it means a lot, and you are supposed to do your best. And yes, you have a responsibility to use your talent. So do the best you can, and then forget about it!

After pitching a bad game, I would lie awake and replay every pitch and criticize myself unmercifully. Now I replay pitches, pull out the *positive* things, and use them to do better the next time.

If you think you have the talent to play baseball, never give up. I was never thought of as a pro prospect because I was considered to be too small. But I knew I had a good arm and always figured I would play in the big leagues one day. To help me make it, I tried to get the best possible coaching and to hang around the right guys and the best athletes who were doing the right things. When I got into the minor leagues, I spent my time with the number-one draft choices and guys I thought were going to make it instead of the men who were always partying and not getting their rest. Always listen to the coach, and be the type of person he likes to work with.

There are several Christians on the Dodgers, and we make ourselves part of the whole team. We don't compromise our morals, and the other guys don't expect us to. I really believe if you are consistent in your Bible study and prayer life, others are going to recognize what you have and realize it's something they want.

Don't think you can ever take your eyes off Christ and slack off in your relationship with Him. At one point in my career in AA ball, I was told that I was going to be the next player called up to the majors.

I had a 0.60 ERA and had given up only 2 runs in two months of pitching. I started listening to them and put my faith in what they were saying and not in Christ who got me there. In my next 3 starts, I pitched a total of one inning (3 outs) and gave up 26 runs. My ERA went from 0.60 to 8.60. Everybody thought I had totally lost it mentally and physically. However, I knew what had happened. I had stopped studying my Bible, and my prayer life was almost down to nothing. It was as if the Lord were saying, "Remember Me?"

When we won the divisional title in 1985, I don't think anybody expected us to have losing seasons in 1986 and 1987. And with all of the players we lost to injuries in the World Series, nobody expected to even stay with the A's. So I was just trying to stay relaxed in that fifth game. I was trying to convince myself that it was another game. Maybe I haven't even realized yet that it was more than that.

But I wanted very badly to win it for the players because nobody believed we could do it. So in the clubhouse after we'd finally won when they gave me the MVP trophy I held it real high and showed the other 24 players and yelled, "Hey, guys, this is for you!"

So remember, the Christian life is a walk, not a run. If you fall down, you can get back up whenever you're ready. He's always there.

GARY CARTER
New York Mets/Catcher

"Christ First, My Family Second, And Baseball Third"

When I started putting Christ first in my priorities, my life really began to go in the right direction. Since I'm a professional baseball player, it's easy to put baseball first and my relationships with Jesus Christ and my family whenever I find the time. But I've learned that these three most important things in my life must be kept in order if I'm to succeed in any of them.

I haven't always had these as my goals in life. I was a pretty good kid while growing up in southern California. My mother died when I was twelve, and I really questioned why a loving God would take someone away as dear as Mom. From that time on, I focused everything on sports.

My dad became my biggest supporter, encouraging me to do my very best in everything I tried. I was voted Scholastic Athlete of the Year at Sunnyhills High School in Fullerton, California, and graduated from there in 1972. I was the captain of the baseball, basketball, and football teams,

as well as being a member of the National Honor Society and graduating in the top 50 of my class of 550. I was a high-school All-American quarterback and had signed a letter of intent to play football at UCLA. I was also the third player drafted by the Montreal Expos in June 1972. That's when I decided to play baseball and not football.

I spent only two years in the minors, but it was there that I made the greatest discovery of my life. I went to spring training in 1973, and a pitcher for the Expos named John Boccabella sort of took me under his wing. He was a Christian, and he got me going to church with him and started answering my questions about religion. I saw in John an inner peace and happiness that I wanted, and he said it could only come through a personal relationship with Jesus Christ.

A few weeks later I was sent back to the minors, which seemed to be a setback for me. One night while lying in bed, I just started talking to the Lord and told Him I needed Him and wanted Him to be my personal Savior. I also told Him I wanted to live for Him and be able to share His Word. As I look back now, I realize it was the greatest decision of my life.

Since I've become a Christian, my life hasn't been a bed of roses. I've gone through some tough injuries that have caused me to doubt His wisdom, but those injuries have always brought me closer to Him, and I can truly thank Him for them.

God has allowed me to have some tremendous moments during my baseball career. In 1975 I was named *The Sporting News*'s Rookie of the Year and the Expos Player of the Year. I've been on the All-Star team eight times. In 1981 I hit 2 home runs in the All-Star Game at Cleveland and was named the MVP. Then in 1984, I hit a home run against Dave Stieb and was named the MVP in that All-Star Game. I also hit 2 grand slams in 1985, bringing my career total to 9. I've been able to catch at least 100 games a season for the last nine years, which is third best for a major-league career behind Bill Dickey of the Yankees and the Reds' Johnny Bench, who both did it thirteen years.

In December 1984, I was traded to the New York Mets, and I'm really having a good time catching such great pitchers as Dwight Gooden and Ron Darling. I finished my first season there hitting 32 homers and driving in 100 runs. I finished fifth in the league in homers, tied for sixth in RBI's, tied for second with Dave Parker of the Reds with 18 game-winning RBI's, and was tenth in slugging percentage at .488. Then, to come from behind and win the 1986 World Series with the Red Sox was the icing on the cake of my career thus far!

If a kid really wants to be a good athlete, there is no substitute for hard work. Practice was just pounded into my head when I was growing up. And the attitude you have about practice must be very positive. I know I've been blessed with the ability to play baseball, but I also believe that I have to continue to work at it. Whenever I think I've reached a plateau where I know it all, that's when I start going downhill. There is always something more you can learn about anything.

I also think it is very important for young people to have role models or adults to look up to. Jesus Christ is the ultimate model, but it helps to have someone to look up to here on this earth, too. In my generation everybody really watched Mickey Mantle, and I think you should pick out someone you respect and would like to be like. Then find out how that adult got to be the person he is and how you can do the same things.

I have really been fortunate to have been successful in my baseball career. I know that having the Lord in my heart has freed me up inside so I can strive to be the best I can be. Knowing the Lord is going to be there in the bad times and the good gives me all the support I need, because I know that wherever I am, He's going to be there, too.

DWIGHT EVANS
Boston Red Sox/Outfielder

"No Oral Book Report; I'll Take An 'F'"

When I was nine years old, my family moved from Hawaii to Chatsworth, California. I had never played any kind of ball until we moved there. Softball was the game I picked up first, and I learned to play it pretty fast. The next year I started Little League and found that I loved playing baseball more than going to the beach. Playing baseball became a way of life for me, and everything I did revolved around it.

I've always been very shy. I'll never forget one time in junior high school when I was supposed to give an oral book report. I had the report written in my notebook, and the teacher called on me to stand up and read it. To keep from having to give it orally, I told her I didn't have it. She said that if that were true, I'd get an "F." I took the "F." I was that shy and terrified of having to stand up in front of the class.

I have great memories of growing up in Chatsworth. Our family was not real close, however, because my father had to travel a lot. There

were seven of us, and we were always very competitive around the dinner table. I really appreciated my grandfather David Lionel Evans. He had a nice ranch near Chatsworth, and he would pay me for plowing his orange groves. That was something special for a twelve-year-old boy to get to drive a tractor all the time. My grandfather would always let me off and take me to my ball games. He never really taught me about baseball or sports, but he was always there to talk to me or motivate me to do my best.

In Little, Colt, Pony, and Connie Mack leagues in Northridge, California, I was an All-Star just about every year. I made the All-League team playing third base and was the MVP at Chatsworth High School. After graduation in 1969, I signed with the

Boston Red Sox, who had drafted me in the fifth round. I spent almost four years in the minors before the Red Sox called me up, and I've been in the majors ever since.

I've enjoyed thirteen years with the Red Sox and have won eight Gold Glove Awards while playing right field. I've played in three All-Star Games and three World Series. I guess the most exciting time in baseball for me was in the 1975 World Series against the Cincinnati Reds. I hit a home run in the ninth inning of one game and made a key catch. We lost the Series in 7 games, but it was still very exciting just to be there. Then in the 1986 World Series, we were up 3 games to 2, and we lost it in 7. That last game was a tough loss, but now I have to forget about it and look forward to next season.

I really do love baseball, but you know, it's not the most important thing in my life. That would be my relationship with Jesus Christ. My best friend is my wife, Susan, and together we have been through many tough times that my baseball career could not solve. We had two sons born with serious diseases that were miraculously healed. It was during those times that we turned our lives over to Christ. Our older son had a brain tumor the size of a quarter that completely disappeared. The doctors still wonder how it happened so quickly. We know how it happened; it was God's healing. But you know, even if God had not healed our sons, we would still love and serve Him, because we know now how much He loves us and wants to give us the best life we can possibly have. I love His promise in 1 Corinthians 10:13, in which He tells us He'll never give us more problems than we can handle.

Before a person can be the best he can be in anything, he must establish a growing relationship with the Lord. Then if he still wants to play baseball, he has to work very hard at it and love the game. If you are still in school, take the time needed to study and do your homework right, instead of just rushing through. I'm not always going to be able to play baseball, but I'm going to have to get along in life and use the things I was supposed to learn in school. I took a lot of shortcuts in school, and I'll have to pay for them the rest of my life because I didn't take the time to do it right back then. If you are going to do something, take the time to do it right the first time. That goes for baseball and anything else you do.

JESSE BARFIELD
Toronto Blue Jays/Outfielder

"I Absolutely Crushed That Saberhagen Fastball"

In Game 3 of the 1985 American League Championship Series against Kansas City, I had a phenomenal game. Defensively, I made catches in the outfield that I never thought possible, and offensively, I hit the ball as hard as I can. Bret Saberhagen threw me a fastball that I absolutely crushed over the right-field fence. The only reason I didn't get Player of the Game was that George Brett had an even better game. I ended the Series batting .280, with 1 home run and 4 RBI's. In the 1986 season I was fortunate to lead the Major Leagues in home runs.

My baseball career and most of my life have been a series of ups and downs, mostly downs until I made a startling discovery. I'll tell you what changed my life after I tell you a little bit about my past.

I am the oldest of four children, with two brothers and a sister. I was raised in a broken home, but I sure have to give a lot of credit to my mom for

bringing us up and keeping us together. Growing up in Joliet, Illinois, was a lot of fun because it was so close to the big city of Chicago. I always liked baseball, and Chicago is a big baseball town with the Cubs and White Sox playing there.

I remember working hard and making a lot of sacrifices to play baseball at Joliet Central High School. There's a lot of tradition in Joliet for baseball because major leaguers Bill Gullickson and Jack Perconte played in Joliet, as well as former major leaguer Larry Gura. All the hard work paid off for me when I was named to the All-Conference team and was selected First Team All-American in my senior year, 1977. Then it really paid off when I was selected in the ninth round in June of that same year by the Toronto Blue Jays.

I stayed in the minor leagues for four years and finally in 1981 was called up to the majors for a short time near the end of the season. In 1982 I made the parent team for good and have been in the majors ever since.

I'll never forget my first time at bat in the big leagues. I was lucky enough to get a hit, an RBI, and a stolen base against the White Sox in a game played near my hometown. Three days later I got my first home run, which was also a thrill. I set a club rookie record, which still stands, for hitting safely in 8 straight games at the start of my career.

I was really living life in the fast lane with money, cars, and big houses, yet my career started going downhill fast. At the beginning of the season in 1982, I was so miserable because of all the partying and lack of rest, and I knew I had to make a change. Roy Lee Jackson was a pitcher for the Blue Jays at that time, and he was a born-again Christian. He really had his act together, and a bad performance didn't bother him the way it did the rest of us. He would talk to me from time to time and just put his arm around me and encourage me. He started inviting me to Bible studies, but I always found an excuse not to go. One day he invited me along with teammates Lloyd Moseby and Al Wood. I took my girlfriend, Marla, who is now my wife, and we went to his apartment and listened to a cassette tape on the subject of hell. He then explained that I was headed for hell unless I accepted God's gift of salvation. I had never had the Gospel explained so clearly to me before. That day Marla and I both invited Christ into our lives. It is a day that means more to us than any home run I'll ever be able to hit!

That day we may have accepted Christ for what some people call "fire insurance," but since then we have come to realize how much God loves us and how empty our lives were before Him.

Some people think Christians are passive and have no get-up-and-go. A reporter interviewed me after my team had just lost the American League Championship Series in 1985, and we were talking about why people have this idea. I had just had a fantastic year and a great Series play-off that included some of the most aggressive baseball I have ever played. I asked him if he thought I was passive, and he replied, "I think not." I play that way now more easily because I'm not playing for myself. I'm playing for the glory of God, and He judges my performance on how much I put out, not whether I win or lose. With Him I'm always a winner.

SCOTT FLETCHER
Texas Rangers/Infielder

"Wadsworth, Ohio, Home Of The Grizzlies"

Wadsworth, Ohio, is a small town outside of Akron where I grew up and went to high school. It was known as "The Home of the Grizzlies," our school mascot. Our family consisted of me and my brother and our parents. Mom was a nurse, and Dad was a former minor-league ballplayer who has since been a coach at the high-school and college levels. While he was in the minors, I hung around the ballpark a lot. Since he was a high-school coach, he naturally encouraged and helped me develop my skills in baseball.

I became a Christian at a Billy Graham Crusade along with my brother and mother when I was thirteen. I remembered the invitation at the end of his sermon from television, and I thought everybody always went down front. My dad stayed in his seat that night, however, but later he accepted Christ on his own. I rededicated my life to the Lord when I was a senior and realized God wanted all of my life.

I graduated from Wadsworth High School in 1976 and was drafted by the Los Angeles Dodgers. I decided I wanted to play college ball first, though, and went to Valencia, Florida, Junior College. While still in school, I was drafted by the Oakland A's and by the Houston Astros. I was also named Junior College Player of the Year and All-Florida Division II shortstop in 1978. I then transferred to Georgia Southern College in Statesboro, Georgia. We went to the NCAA Atlantic Regional Tournament, and I ended the year batting .461. After that season, I was drafted by the Chicago Cubs in 1979 and started my pro career.

I was traded to the Chicago White Sox and finally got up to the big leagues in 1983. That was my rookie season, and we played the Baltimore Orioles for the American League pennant. I didn't do too well, nor did the White Sox, but it was a great thrill just to be there, especially in my rookie season. A big-league ballplayer never forgets his first major-league hit. Mine came off Sparky Lyle, and my first home run was off Lenny Whitehouse. Those times really stand out when you've dreamed all your life of playing major-league baseball.

I also got married in 1983, and my wife, Angie, is a real source of inspiration for me. She's also a Christian, and together we are growing spiritually day by day.

A person who really wants to play professional baseball is going to have to learn discipline and develop good work habits. He's going to have to love the game and be willing to pay the price to get to the top. That means sacrificing now, to get a good payoff later. These principles have to be developed at an early age. I remember going to a hot, muggy baseball field in the summer and hitting and chasing the balls I'd hit all day, while the other kids were going swimming. Nothing that's worth doing comes easy.

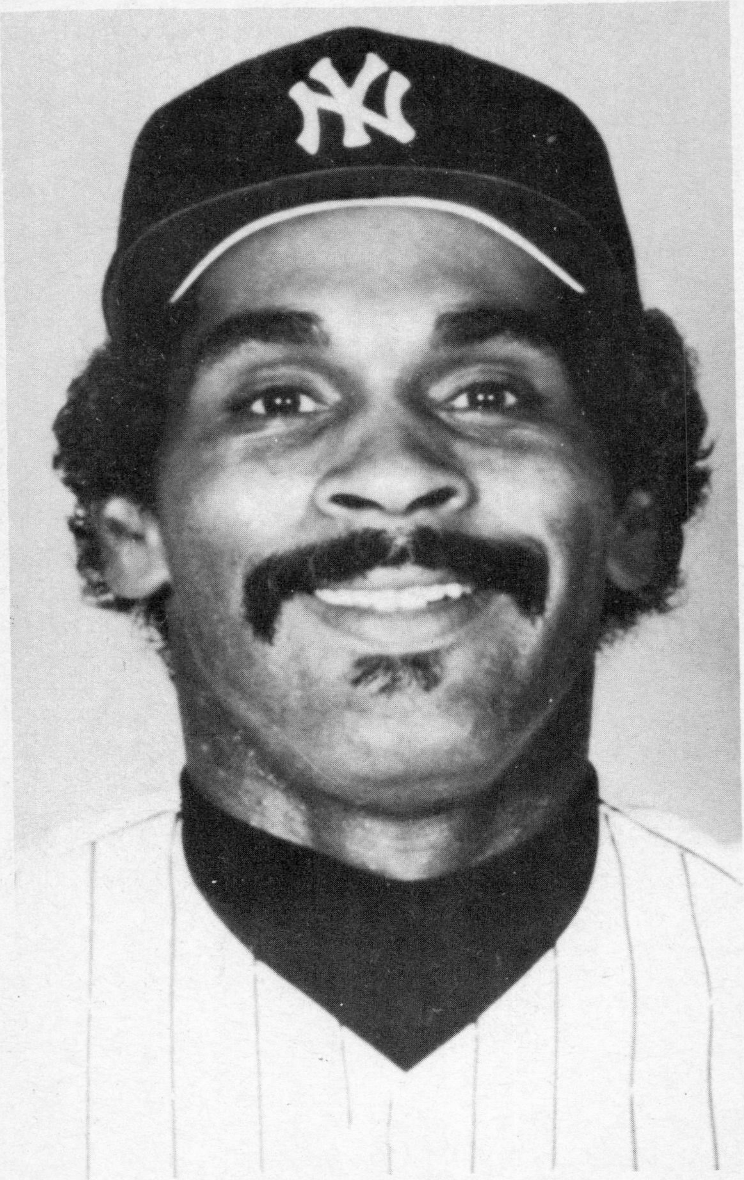
NY

MIKE EASLER
Philadelphia Phillies/First Baseman & Outfielder

"Come On, Coach, Let Me Bat!"

It was the bottom of the thirteenth inning, and I was about the last player left on the bench. I was playing for the Pittsburgh Pirates against the Mets and started bugging my batting coach, Bob Skinner, to tell the manager to let me bat. I wasn't getting through to him, so I started hitting my bat against the wall in the dugout. Finally, I think Coach Skinner thought I was a little crazy, and he told the manager to bat me just to get me off his back. I walked up to the plate and promptly hit the first pitch over the right-field wall for a game-winning home run. That started a 9-game winning streak for us, and that year we went on to win the 1979 World Series.

It's too bad problems in life can't be solved as easily as hitting a home run in baseball. I grew up in a happy family of nine brothers and sisters. Mom and Dad really did a super job of giving us everything we needed—not everything we wanted, but everything we needed. My parents were both from

© Yankees Magazine

broken families, and they were determined to
stand together and give us all their love and support. Dad worked two jobs and still found the time
to encourage me athletically by playing with me in
the driveway or the park. And then when I was in
Little League and high-school ball games, he was
always there. I think he wanted to live out his
dream of playing ball through me.

I went to a Catholic grade school and graduated
from Benedictine High School in Cleveland, Ohio.
While I was in high school, baseball was my main
game, and I made All-City three years and All-State
once as a pitcher and third baseman. I also lettered in football twice as a halfback.

I was drafted in the fourteenth round by the
Houston Astros, and the scout said I wouldn't

make it through the first week of rookie baseball. He didn't want to give me any money for signing, but I just had to have something to be able to feel good about myself and tell my friends about. So after much debate, I received a small bonus for signing with the Astros. I ended up getting about five hundred dollars, and I started with a strike against me that seemed to last my whole minor-league career.

I spent ten years of my life in the minor leagues. That's a whole lot longer than most major-league ballplayers put in there, and I probably would have quit if it hadn't been for an experience I had in spring training at Cocoa Beach in 1975 and the love of my father and wife and mom. Astro stars Bob Watson and Dave Roberts—along with a lady who had given me an article that spoke of my need to receive Christ—had been talking to me about spiritual things. At that point in my life I was ready to listen to anything. They invited me to Baseball Chapel, and right there in the training complex I prayed to receive Jesus Christ as my personal Savior.

After that happened I made the major leagues for the first time, but I was devastated when I got sent back down to the minors. I more or less asked God, "Why me?" However, this time in the minor leagues was different. I knew I was going to make it back to the majors. God had given me a new confidence that I was in His will and exactly where He wanted me to be. I bounced up and down between the majors and minors for a couple more years until I got traded to Pittsburgh, and I've been in the major leagues ever since.

Hitting a home run to win a game, playing in the World Series, and hitting for the cycle (single, double, triple, and home run in one game) are all great experiences. But the highs they create go away, and you have to come back down to reality. A relationship with Jesus Christ is something that will always be there to pick you up when you're down and to give you purpose when you're up *or* down. Being a Christian has given me a confidence and peace that is not available anywhere else. I used to worry for days about why I didn't get that hit or why I made that error. Now, when I fall short, I learn from it and then forget about it and move on.

If I were asked to give advice to young people about what I would do differently if I were eleven years old again, I would say first get to know Christ. That has to be the starting point. Without Him you'll never be as good as you could be and you'll never know what you're supposed to be in this life. Second, obey your parents without asking so many questions. If they're like most parents, they really love you and want and know what's best for you. Third, as you get into high school, make an assessment of your talents and abilities and ask God and your parents to help you choose what you should do. And last, don't spend much time with people who don't believe what you do. Most of the time they'll hurt you more than you can help them.

This past year I was licensed to be a minister. Now I'm a minister and a *professional ballplayer*. I have a wonderful wife and three beautiful daughters. Professional baseball is tough on a family. We bought a house in one city and two months later I was traded to another team in another city. Last year in spring training, I hit a 2-run homer off Dwight Gooden, and that night while traveling to speak to a youth group, I was traded to the Yankees after being with the Boston Red Sox for two years. If I based my life on my baseball career, I would be a complete wreck, but I base my life on my relationship with Christ. I especially like John 14:27, which says, "Peace I leave with you, My peace I give to you; not as the world gives do I give to you. Let not your heart be troubled, neither let it be afraid." My peace comes from Christ, not base-ball.

My peace is consistent because Christ is consistent, and He doesn't lie. And because of that, I'll play baseball wherever I'm supposed to play as long as I'm supposed to play. And then I'll just do what the Lord has for me next. I'm His vessel to use and to glorify His precious and holy name. Jesus is alive and well, and He can be alive in your life too. Just ask Him into your life by faith, and you will be a new creature in Christ.

TOM HERR
St. Louis Cardinals/Second Baseman

"Why Do The Dodgers Always Beat The Giants?"

I grew up in a small town in eastern Pennsylvania and was an avid San Francisco Giants fan. I lived and died with the fortunes of the Giants and Willie Mays, Willie McCovey, and Juan Marichal. During my high-school years, they were always in a dogfight with the Dodgers, and they seemed to come up short every year. It's amazing how much I poured myself into each of those games and how crazy I went every time the Giants would lose.

There were four of us in my family, and were we ever sports nuts! My brother, who is four years older than I am, and I played everything we could get our hands on. My whole purpose in life was to be playing some kind of ball. I guess that carried over into my high-school years, because I earned eleven letters in four sports before graduating from Hempfield High School in Landisville, Pennsylvania. I also was named to the All-League team two years in succession, in 1973 and 1974, in base-

ball as a second baseman and shortstop. I was the MVP in the Legion All-East Pennsylvania All-Star Game as well as the Eastern Pennsylvania Regional Championship. I guess you could say baseball was my best game.

I signed a professional contract with the St. Louis Cardinals as a free agent right out of high school in 1974. I spent almost six years in the minor leagues before I finally made it to the majors. It was during my stay in the minor leagues that I realized there had to be more to life than baseball. I had grown up in the church and attended every Sunday, but I still didn't know who Jesus Christ was or what to do with Him. I was twenty years old when I found out that being a good guy and a nice person was not getting me anywhere. The thing I had put all my faith in, baseball, had failed me, and I had to find something better to base my life on.

After I became a Christian, life didn't get easier, but I was able to handle the pressures because of my newfound faith. It was still another four years of hard work and determination before the Lord allowed me to make the majors. However, those years in the minors taught me how to be the ballplayer I am today and, most of all, the confident person I am in Jesus Christ.

I've been fortunate to have been in the major leagues for several years now and to have played in two World Series. In 1982 we came back from a 2–3 deficit in games to beat the Milwaukee Brewers and bring the world championship trophy back to St. Louis for the first time in fifteen years. I set a World Series record in Game 4 when two players scored on my long sacrifice fly.

Until 1985 the highlight of my career was being on that world championship team. But 1985 was my best year ever in the majors. I was ninth in the league in batting average, eighth in runs scored, ninth in hits, third in doubles, third in RBI's, sixth in game-winning hits, tenth in walks, and eighth in on-base percentage. I also hit a home run in the top of the ninth inning with two outs to win a game against Montreal. It was disappointing not winning the Series against the Royals, but that's baseball. You give it all you have, and if you come up short, you remember it's a game.

I think that's something to remember as a young person playing ball. Work hard by listening to your coaches and developing the best skills you possibly can. But most of all, learn to have fun and not take the game too seriously. Don't ever think you are a failure if you don't get that big hit in a clutch situation. If you are trying your best, you'll never be a failure, even when you lose a ballgame.

BILL RUSSELL
Los Angeles Dodgers/Infielder

"A Dodger For Sixteen Years"

It's hard to believe I was in the major leagues for sixteen years, and all of them with the Dodgers. As a matter of fact, before my recent retirement I had been with the same team longer than any other active player in professional baseball. I played in five League Championship Series with a combined batting average of .337, plus four World Series, and three All-Star Games. I guess that's not bad for a boy from a small town in Kansas whose high school didn't even have a baseball team!

I grew up with two older brothers and two younger sisters in Pittsburg, Kansas. I was really the only one, except for my sisters, interested in athletics. My main sport in high school was basketball, and I signed a letter of intent to play college basketball. I played baseball just in the summers so I was really surprised to get drafted by the Dodgers in June 1966. That's the first time I ever realized that I might be able to play pro baseball. I spent about four years in the minors before I made it up to the Dodgers for good in 1970.

In 1977 an event happened that really changed my life. As a boy, I had always gone to church and heard the preachers preach, but I couldn't wait to get out of church and play ball. As a young adult, I stopped going to church. Even after I married Mary Anne, who was a regular churchgoer, I didn't go. When we had children, she took them to church with her, but I didn't join them. My pattern of *not* attending church was predictable, to say the least. But things changed while we were living in Broken Arrow, Oklahoma. One of our neighbors was bugging me about going to a revival service at her church. I was getting tired of her nagging me, so I thought, *What the heck. I'll go just to get her off my back.* It wasn't that I didn't believe in Jesus, but I had never really taken the time to consider what it meant to follow Him. I also had some wrong ideas about churches. I thought churches were just places where they always asked for money and told you what you *couldn't* do. Boy, was I wrong about a lot of things. That night I invited Christ into my life, and I received a peace that has stayed with me ever since.

I had some big hits in my career. In the League Championship Series against the Phillies in 1978, I drove in the winning run in the tenth inning of the final game to give us our second National League pennant in a row. I guess the thing I am most proud of is being able to come back from two injuries that could have ended my career. In 1981 my right index finger was shattered, and you certainly can't play much baseball without that finger, especially when you throw right-handed. It's amazing the complete peace I had during that time—I knew I would be back playing again. I never had any doubts, even when the doctor and everyone else did.

It's a real shame the way kids today have so much pressure put on them at an early age to win. Instead of learning to win at all costs, youngsters should be taught to develop their skills and the confidence they need to have. My last manager on the Dodgers, Tommy Lasorda, said one day in practice that we as pro baseball players are really fortunate to be getting paid for something we used to do all day for nothing. I always had fun practicing, and there is just no substitute for it. I don't care what your job may be, if you don't enjoy it and have fun with it, you'll never be successful.

SCOTT McGREGOR
Baltimore Orioles/Pitcher

*"It Was The World Series, And I Was
Sweating Bullets"*

In the 1983 World Series, I experienced what the
word *pressure* really means. We were leading the
Philadelphia Phillies 3–1 in the best-of-7 Series. It
was the night before Game 5, and I was due to
pitch. My team had been in this same situation in
the '79 Series with the Pittsburgh Pirates. We had
been up 3–1, only to lose 3 straight games and the
title. I had been the losing pitcher in the seventh
and deciding game that year, and people thought
we were going to choke again and lose this Series,
too.

During the twenty-four hours before that fifth
game in 1983, I think I literally wrestled with the
devil. I had never had so many negative thoughts
go through my mind. Then about one in the morning, God led me to read some verses out of the
Bible found in Philippians chapter 3. Paul was talking about counting all things as loss compared to
knowing Christ. I had to count that next game as a
loss. God showed me that anything I would gain

from winning that game would be garbage in comparison to what He has for me in His kingdom. I prayed and thanked Him and got some sleep the rest of the night.

The next day I went out to pitch Game 5 of the '83 World Series with the whole world watching and peace in my heart, knowing that it didn't matter whether I won or lost the game. I did just happen to pitch a 5-hit shutout, however, and we won the World Series with a 5–0 victory. Reporters commented after the game that they had noticed a peace that everyone could see. And I knew where that peace came from.

I had not always handled pressure that way. Growing up in El Segundo, California, the same town George and Ken Brett grew up in, was a great experience. George and I played on the same El Segundo High School team, where I was 51–5 and had a 0.029 ERA in four seasons. Playing in that atmosphere was great, but I really have to give a lot of credit to my older brother for helping me get to where I am today. He broke his elbow in a bicycle accident and then became my backyard catcher. Without him I wouldn't have made it this far.

In 1972 I was drafted by the New York Yankees in the first round and went straight to their big-league spring training camp in Ft. Lauderdale, Florida. I had a great spring training but was sent down to their AAA team in Syracuse, N.Y., shortly before camp ended. In Syracuse, I won 10 of my first 11 decisions while posting a 1.70 ERA. Everyone, including my pitching coach, Cloyd Boyer, expected me to be called up to the big leagues at any moment. I was left-handed and the Yankees needed a lefty, so I was the obvious choice. But the call never came, and instead the Yankees traded for veteran left-hander Rudy May. That's when I really got bummed out with baseball. My baseball ability really just started to leave me. I was all tied up with a lot of little strings like Gulliver, the giant in the book *Gulliver's Travels*. When you're down, a lot of little things can get to you and tie you up and frustrate you.

In 1976 the Yankees traded me to the Orioles. I was just a .500 pitcher at that point, and I'm sure the Yankees thought I couldn't make it. They were right, too; I can't disagree with their decision one bit.

After I joined the Orioles, I met Pat Kelly, an outfielder with the Orioles whose lifestyle and testimony made me face God and His reality. In the minors my coach, Cloyd Boyer, first showed me what living with Christ was all about. God had placed Christians in my path who really made me think about Him. Pat was just beginning His walk with Christ, and I had never seen someone so unashamed and excited about religion. He really caught my attention, and I started going to his chapel meeting before our games.

Then during a chapel service in 1979, I realized I couldn't turn my back on all the peace and joy that had been unfolded through the Bible to me. That day I invited Christ to come into my life. From that moment baseball became fun again, just like playing when I was growing up.

My game since then has greatly improved. Among active pitchers, I have one of the best won-lost percentages in the major leagues. I've been selected to an All-Star team and played in two World Series. During my time with the Orioles, we have only experienced one losing season.

In sports, you are only as good as your last game. I can remember right after we won the '83 Series getting on the bus and hearing a fan shout, "Now you have to do it again next year." We had just won the World Series a couple hours earlier, and already they wanted us to do it again! No one is ever satisfied in this game.

When I made it to the major leagues, I thought everything was going to be great—you know, no bills, no worries. It wasn't that way the least bit. You have to have something that will keep your feet on the ground. And that something is Jesus Christ. God has given us all some ability, and we have to dedicate ourselves to being the best we can be and then letting God take care of the rest. The best things any person can do are to commit oneself and one's talents to the Lord, get to know Him and His Word, and then enjoy life.

JIM SUNDBERG
Kansas City Royals/Catcher

"Six Gold Glove Awards And Three All-Star Games"

After six Gold Glove Awards and three All-Star Games, I finally tasted post-season action in 1985 for the first time in my long major-league career. And did I ever enjoy it! In the American League Championship Series, I led the club with 6 RBI's. I hit a bases-loaded triple off the top of the right-field fence in Game 7 that broke open the game and helped us to claim the American League pennant. That hit completed the cycle (single, double, triple, and home run) for me in the Series.

Then came the World Series against the St. Louis Cardinals. The Cardinals were ahead in the Series, 3–1. I had a hit and scored 2 runs as we won Game 5 to stay alive and avoid elimination. Then came the unforgettable Game 6. We were behind, 0–1, and the Cardinals had never lost a game in 1985 when they were leading going into the ninth inning. Dane Iorg came to bat after a controversial call at first base and a couple of Cardinal errors had left Onix Concepcion on third base and

me on second with one out. Dane was a pinch hit-
ter with a lot of pressure on him, but he hit a single
to right field and I was able to score the winning
run. Our momentum carried over into Game 7 as
we won 11–0 to become the world champions.

I realize how fortunate I am to have played in a
World Series, because some guys play their whole
careers and only see the Series from the stands.
And if their lives are built around baseball, they will
feel they have never been a success. I'm happy to
say that even if I had never made it to the World
Series, because of who I am in Jesus Christ, I can
always be a success.

I haven't always felt that way, because I used to
have my life centered on baseball. As I grew up in
Illinois, my father used to pitch batting practice to

me at least once a week. After I graduated from Galesburg High School in 1969, I was drafted by the Oakland A's in the fourteenth round. Dad helped me decide to accept a baseball scholarship at the University of Iowa, where we won the 1971 Big Ten Championship. That same year I made the All-American team. In 1973 I was selected in the second round of the draft by the Texas Rangers and was sent to the minor leagues. I played only 91 minor-league games before becoming the regular catcher of the Rangers in 1974. When I got to the majors, I had the attitude that this was the ultimate and I had arrived. I thought playing professional baseball would bring me all the peace, joy, and happiness I could handle. In my fourth year of baseball, I had been to the All-Star Game and was making more money than I knew what to do with. And yet, I was so miserable! Then in 1977, after feeling total frustration and realizing baseball was not satisfying my needs for peace and joy, I finally asked Jesus Christ to come into my life and take control of it. Then I went through the worst three years of my life. It was my own fault. I thought that after I gave my life to Christ, things would just automatically get better. I didn't realize that if God is going to direct your life, you have to listen to what He has to say. And the way He speaks to most people is through His Word, the Bible. I didn't get into Bible study until 1981, and then I really found out all I had as a believer and could have had for the past three years if I had just been studying His Word.

Young people today really have a tough time with peer pressure. As I look back, I think that was my greatest problem about growing up. I have a teen-age son, and it's a problem for him, too. I think the best way to fight bad peer pressure is to surround yourself with friends who have the right attitudes and ideas that you know you should have. People are stronger in groups, and when you're growing up, it's very difficult to stand on your own. As a person grows older and more mature from being among the right friends, the stronger his self-image will become, and it will be more difficult for him to be swayed by rejection and peer pressure. You have to be strong about who you are and where you're going.

If you really like baseball and want to be the best you can be, here's what I would do. From Little League through high school, play as many positions as you possibly can. Work hard in practice and always hustle, because that really impresses the scouts. Be coachable and willing to try whatever the coach tells you to do. Never be cocky. Nobody likes to play with or coach someone who thinks he's great, even if he is.

Playing in an All-Star Game and the World Series was a lot of fun and a great experience. However, these events are not the greatest things in the world. After reading my story, you know what I think will bring you the only real peace and joy available. If you agree with me, keep growing and doing what God wants you to do. If you don't agree, think about it, and then do what you know you should.

GLENN HUBBARD
Atlanta Braves/Second Baseman

"Keeper Of 'The Dead Zone'"

In 1980, the Braves brought me up from the minors for the last time, and I've been the regular second baseman ever since. In 1985, I led all major-league second basemen in total chances (888), assists (539), and double plays (127) while playing in 142 games. Just 5 games into the season, on April 14, I tied a major-league record for assists in a game by a second baseman when I had 12 against the San Diego Padres. My teammates began calling the area around second base "The Dead Zone."

I have to give my father a lot of credit for my being in the major leagues today. He always took time out to practice with me and encouraged me in every way to learn the game. I was an Air Force "brat" born in West Germany. I played Little League baseball in Taiwan and many other places because we moved around a lot. Dad realized there was good money in baseball, so he told me to concentrate on the game and play all summer and

he would take care of what money I needed. I had four brothers and one sister and a solid home life.

I went to high school in Ogden, Utah, and was a four-sport letterman while participating in basketball, football, and wrestling as well as baseball. I was named the MVP twice in the state All-Star baseball game and received the award as the Most Inspirational Wrestler at Ben Lomand High, from which I graduated in 1975.

The Braves drafted me right out of high school in the twentieth round and sent me to Kingsport, Tennessee. I was in the minors for three years before being called up to Atlanta the first time. I was sent back down to AAA ball in Richmond, Virginia, two more times before I made the team for good.

It was during my time in the minors that I learned what life is all about. In 1977 when I was playing for the Greenwood Braves, I met this beautiful waitress in a Pizza Hut. Shortly after that I was sent up to AA ball, but I went back to Greenwood at the end of the season to see them in the play-offs. After one of the games, I saw this same girl again, and she asked me if I needed a ride. Of course I said yes, thinking I had it made for the night. As we were riding around, she asked if I would like to see the plants in her house. I thought she just wanted to get me to her place, so I said yes again. Once we were in her house, she said she needed to go into her bedroom for a few moments, and I thought that was just great! A little later she came out of her bedroom with a Bible and proceeded to present Christ and the plan of salvation to me! This was something I had never seen in a girl before or since. If she had not had the guts to do that, I would probably still be without Christ today. I asked Him to come into my life that winter in Instructional League on a beach in Sarasota, Florida.

And, boy, was that perfect timing for what was going on in my life. When I was in Greenwood, I had three Christian roommates who were telling me about Jesus, but I was hitting .385 and didn't think I needed Him. When I moved up to AA ball, my roommates there liked to party and stay out late, and my average dipped to .220. So when that girl told me about this personal relationship with Christ, I was ready. Oh, by the way, I married that Pizza Hut waitress, Lynn, and we now have three sons.

There are three outstanding things in my career that I will always remember. First, I was a part of the Braves team that had the 13-game winning streak. At the end of that thirteenth game, people ran out on the field as though we had just won the World Series. They were trying to tear our clothes off and steal our hats and gloves. It sure was a big thrill for me. The second was being part of the youngest triple play in the major leagues. There were runners on first and second, and Jose Cardenal of the Phillies hit a two hopper to third-baseman Bob Horner. He stepped on third, then threw to me on second, and I threw to Dale Murphy who was on first for a triple play. It was Horner (twenty years old) to me (twenty years old) to Murphy (twenty-two years old). And then third, I made the All-Star team in 1983 and got a hit.

Life doesn't become a bed of roses when you become a Christian. You have to remember that something as beautiful as a rose also has thorns, and you have to learn to take the good with the bad. But as a Christian, when you realize that even the bad will turn out for your good (see Romans 8:28), it makes the bad not so bad after all.

FRANK TANANA
Detroit Tigers/Pitcher

"All-Star Team, #1 In Strikeouts, #1 In ERA, Still Empty Inside!"

After five years in the majors and being single, I had experienced all that life had to offer. I had lots of money, expensive cars, and a big house, yet inside I was so empty and dissatisfied. Sure I liked the awards and praise, but after a few days, it was all over and I had to move on to try to find a higher "high." *There has to be more to life than this,* I said to myself.

My father was a police officer in Detroit and had played baseball in the minor leagues with the Cleveland Indians organization, so he was always there to encourage me. He and Mom were just great keeping me and my three younger sisters healthy and giving us a solid home life. They put us in good Catholic schools, and I graduated from Detroit Catholic Central High School, where I earned All-State honors in baseball and basketball.

I signed a professional contract with the California Angels just after graduation. They promptly sent me to Idaho Falls, where I spent my first base-

ball season with a bad arm. I was the first-round draft choice of the Angels, so they sent me anyway, and there I played a lot of pepper and developed some pretty good fielding skills. It was a tough year watching guys who could play get cut and me there not playing and still drawing a check just because I was the number-one draft choice. I started drinking while I was there, and I developed some other bad habits I'm not proud of.

I spent two years in the minors, and then in the last part of 1973, I was brought up to the majors and have been there ever since. For the next five years I was very successful as a baseball player. I won the Rookie Pitcher of the Year Award in 1974, I had three successive seasons with over 200 strikeouts, I made the All-Star team three times, and I led the league in 1977 with a 2.54 ERA and 7 shutouts. You would think that would be enough to make anybody happy, but it wasn't. I was miserable!

It was about this time that I met Kathy, whom I later married, and I wanted to change my lifestyle. Then my arm started to bother me, and I was scared to death that my career might be coming to an end.

Fortunately, as all these things were happening I met John Werhas, who led chapel services for the southern California professional sports teams. I had attended baseball chapel on several occasions and saw something in John that I really wanted. You could tell he really cared about you regardless of what you did on or off the field. One day I asked him what made him different from other people I knew. He said it was his relationship with Jesus Christ. I didn't have any idea what he was talking about, so we had lunch together and he explained it to me. At that time I wasn't ready to try it. Then a couple of months later, a good friend of mine, Lyman Bostock, was killed in Gary, Indiana. That really shook me up and made me realize how short life can be and how fast it can be taken away from you.

That fall my wife and I started attending Bible studies and became Christians. To tell you of all the changes that have taken place in my life since then would take more than a book. To state it briefly, baseball is no longer first in my life. As a matter of fact, it's not even second! Baseball is now third in my life behind my relationships with Christ and my family.

If I could live my younger years over again, I would get to know Him as early as possible. Then I would have had real freedom in dealing with pressures that come every day. Being a Christian gives me the assurance that God is in control no matter what happens to my game or anything else. Next, I would do everything with total enthusiasm, discipline, and dedication. I'd play a lot and practice and enjoy competition, but not get carried away because of a "game."

A lot of people would say I am a major-league baseball pitcher today because I had the desire and determination to get here and stay here. And much of what they say is probably true. But I know I'm where I am today because this is where God wants me for now.

CRAIG REYNOLDS
Houston Astros/Shortstop

"I Think I Learned To Walk With A Bat In My Hand"

Growing up with two brothers who were good athletes, I had no choice about whether I would play ball or not. I had one brother ten years older and another five years older, and both saw to it that I participated in every sport available. Houston, Texas, was a great place to grow up, especially since I was the baby of the family and we were always going places. But the thing I really appreciate most is my Christian parents and the right direction they always gave me, even when I thought they didn't quite know as much as they really did.

My grandfather was a minister and my dad was a deacon, so when it came to religion, I always knew what to say and do to make anyone think I was a saint. At a very early age I walked the aisle at church and supposedly became a Christian. After six years of going through the motions, however, I began to question my commitment. I was in the ninth grade, and it was at a youth revival at my church that I was confronted with the fact that I had

to personally accept Christ regardless of what my family had done before me. As I sat there in that seat, I made that commitment once and for all.

I was a pretty good basketball and baseball player in high school. As a matter of fact, I liked basketball more than baseball. One day during my sophomore year, I was playing varsity baseball and the scouts were watching another player on our team, but they also noticed me. After my junior year, I knew I was probably going to be drafted into pro baseball. I remember going on a missions trip with the young people from my church. As a committed Christian, I really wanted to do with my life only what God wanted, and I repeated that prayer again on that trip. I told a good friend of mine what I had prayed, and he jokingly told me there was no way I would be anything but a pro ballplayer. That friend now teaches at Houston Baptist College, and when he said that, it really stuck with me.

One year after that missions trip, in 1971, I graduated from Reagan High School in Houston and was drafted by the Pittsburgh Pirates in the eighth round. I spent several years in the minors before I came up to the big leagues for a short time and was then sent back down. If it hadn't been for my relationship with Christ, I probably would have quit. But I realized that wherever I was sent, that's exactly where God wanted me to be. I came up for good in 1976 and was traded to Seattle. In 1978 I had a pretty good season and was selected to be on the American League All-Star team. At the end of that season, I was traded to Houston for pitcher Floyd Bannister. I made the All-Star team in Houston in 1979 to become one of only a few players to be on the All-Star team in both leagues.

The most exciting experience I've had in baseball was when we won our division in 1980, even though we lost to the Philadelphia Phillies in the play-offs. No one gave us a chance to finish in the upper division, much less win it. However, what I cherish most as an accomplishment in baseball is winning the Danny Thompson award for the most outstanding Christian spirit in professional sports. That award is important to me because trying to be what Christ wants me to be is my goal in life.

I had a rough learning experience when I played in Seattle. For a few months baseball became my god on and off the field. I started to depend on baseball to meet all my needs, and I fell flat on my face. That experience taught me that the best way we learn dependence on God is by failing on our own. It sure is the tough way, but sometimes we have to do it because of our stubbornness. I wouldn't want to go through it again, but I sure wouldn't change what I learned for anything.

The most important thing anyone can do is to put himself in God's hands, completely. I say that not only for youngsters, but for myself. I have only a few years left in baseball, and then I'm going to have to do something else. I said years ago that I would do whatever God wants me to do, and now I realize I have to do that every day. If God had something for me to do besides baseball, I'd be willing to walk away from the game right now. That's the only way I can live at peace with myself.

STORM DAVIS
San Diego Padres/Pitcher

"From Christian High School To The Major Leagues"

I'll never forget my first major-league game. I had just been called up from Rochester, and we were playing the Oakland A's. It was the top of the ninth inning, the score was tied, there were no outs, and the bases were loaded. You talk about pressure, this was it, and I wasn't even normally a relief pitcher. One run scored on a fielder's choice, but I was able to get the three outs without any more damage being done. Welcome to the major leagues!

Coming from a solid Christian home and attending a Christian high school prepared me well for life in the big leagues. My father was my coach, and we worked hard at the game. One way Dad really helped me was in not counting wins and losses as important as what I learned in a game. Oh, we won a lot of games, but that attitude has helped me be a better pitcher now.

I attended University Christian High School in Jacksonville, Florida. While I was there, I had a

42–3 record over three years and struck out 496 batters in 278 innings, with a 0.046 ERA. I was chosen to be on the All-Region and All-Conference teams for three years and was All-State my junior and senior years. I also lettered in football and basketball. I graduated from University Christian in 1979 and was drafted by the Orioles as their sixth pick. I played minor-league ball in Bluefield, West Virginia; Miami, Florida; Charlotte, North Carolina; and Rochester, New York, before being called up to the parent club for good in May 1982.

I became a Christian at a very early age and have been walking with Christ ever since. I have not been as close to the Lord at times as I should have been, but Christians aren't perfect, especially me!

I'm not called Storm because I was wild but because my mother saw the name in a novel and started calling me that on the day I was born. My real name is George Earl Davis, Jr., after my grandfather, but my parents always liked Storm.

If you are a young person and have the dream of being a big-league ballplayer, hold on to it until God closes the door. You have to remember that out of every one hundred ballplayers who sign a professional contract, only seven of them ever make it to the major leagues. Those are pretty slim odds. However, if that's where God wants you, that's where you'll be. If playing baseball is not where God wants you, He's got something better for you that you will be much happier doing.

Someone asked me once how you should pitch to a batter who is a fellow Christian. My wife, Angie, and I were having dinner once with Mike Davis of the Oakland A's and his wife. He gave an answer that I thought was pretty good, and you can apply this to pitching against your friends or anyone you like. He said it's kind of like the cartoon of the sheep dog and the coyote who are good friends and walk off to work together every day. Once on the job, however, they spend the whole day trying to blow each other up, but then they go home together as best of friends. It's the same way in athletics. My job as a pitcher is to get the guy in the other uniform out. And his job is to hit the daylights out of the ball I'm pitching. After our job is over at the end of the game, we can be best of friends again. That doesn't mean that if someone on my team slugs a guy on the other team I'm supposed to start slugging, too. Fighting is never the answer to anything in sports. When you're on the field, compete with all you've got. When the game is over, forget about anything negative and be friends.

My most exciting moment in the major leagues came when I got to start the fourth game of the World Series in 1983, against the Philadelphia Phillies. In the first inning I faced Joe Morgan, Pete Rose, and Mike Schmidt, in that order. And do you know what happened? I struck out all three of them! That was an experience never to be forgotten. I went on to win the game, and we won the Series in 5 games. I have my World Series ring, and I wear it every once in a while. But you know, winning the World Series is not the most important thing in my life. If it were, that thrill would quickly be over, and my life would be a bunch of ups and downs until maybe I get to be in another one.

I just got traded to the San Diego Padres, and it was kind of a surprise! If the most important thing in my life was baseball, I'd probably be down again. Make sure that the most important thing in your life is something that cannot be taken away, a relationship with Jesus Christ.

FRANK PASTORE
Minnesota Twins/Pitcher

"Johnny Bench Ran Out, And I Jumped Up Into His Arms"

I was a rookie with the Cincinnati Reds in 1979, and we were in a dogfight with the Houston Astros for the National League Western Division pennant. It came down to the last 4-game series of the season, which we played against Atlanta in Cincinnati. We had dropped 2 of 3 in Houston, the only victory being my first major-league complete game. Our manager, John McNamara, gave me the ball against Atlanta four days later. We were 2½ games in first place with 4 to play, and a win that night would clinch at least a tie for the division. That night I threw my first major-league shutout! I remember the last out very vividly. Barry Bonnell was batting for the Braves and rocketed a line drive to Ray Knight to end the game. J. B. (Johnny Bench) came running toward the mound, I jumped up into his arms, and all the Reds celebrated on the field. Later that night, the Dodgers beat the Astros to eliminate them. We won the division on my first shutout! What a great memory!

That was several years ago, and a lot has happened since then. My career has been interrupted several times by injuries, and after being in the Reds organization for eleven years, I was released and signed with the Minnesota Twins in early May 1986 as a free agent. I know God is in charge, and He has me just where He wants me.

I grew up in southern California and was always more of a student than an athlete. I was an only child, and my parents were in their forties when I was born, so they were more like grandparents than parents in some ways. I got more encouragement from good grades than baseball, and after high school I was determined to go to Stanford University. Instead, I was drafted by the Reds in the second round in 1975, and at seventeen I made an impulsive decision that had not been seriously considered by my family and friends. I decided to play professional baseball!

I didn't fully realize I had major-league talent until I actually made it to the major leagues. During my four-year stay in the minor leagues, I was never outstanding. In the year prior to making the majors, I had been the number-three starter on the AA farm club. A true prospect? Hardly. And yet, all along I knew I could pitch. I became the Reds' top winner in 1980 with 13 wins, even though I missed six weeks of the season with an injury to a finger on my pitching hand. Then in 1984 I got hit on my right (pitching) elbow by a line drive off the bat of Steve Sax of the Los Angeles Dodgers. It was at this time that the Lord said, "I'll sit this guy down and talk to him. He's ignoring Me. He's wasting his life. It's time he knew." And by His grace I listened.

I realized I had always put my identity into baseball since becoming a pro. I had created a facade made of image, ego, wealth, and fame. My self-worth was based on my most recent baseball game, and it was up and down all the time.

At fourteen years old I had figured there was a God, so I went to church and got baptized. I was recruited by my friends to play baseball at a Catholic high school, so I became a Catholic. In those years I thought I was doing all the right things. I was using the Lord as a good-luck charm, and I thought He was working. I really believe God used that last injury to take away everything I thought was important. Because my life was baseball, I was shattered when it seemed it had been taken from me. All the money, glory, and everything else I thought I wanted was based on my future success in baseball, and now it was gone, along with my identity as a person. So much of Frank Pastore involved baseball that apart from it, Frank Pastore was nothing.

Then one of my teammates, Tommy Hume, invited me to a team Bible study. I had always respected Tommy for his emotional consistency; he was a strong Christian who lived what he talked. At this Bible study a guy named Wendel Deyo found out that I was an avid reader and challenged me to read a few books by C. S. Lewis and Josh McDowell. After reading McDowell's *Evidence That Demands a Verdict,* I realized I had to make a decision. So I said, "Lord, if You are who You say You are, and it looks as though You are, then I believe You." I started attending Bible studies regularly and reading and studying the Bible for myself. My whole world was changed. That injury was the best thing that ever happened to me.

Every baseball player has memories he will never forget. I guess the one that stands out most in my mind came on Johnny Bench Day. In athletics you have many moving moments like the finish line at a marathon, the last-second shot in basketball, or the seventh game of the World Series. On that day in Cincinnati, to see Johnny Bench hit a home run on his day and hear the ovation that followed was the most moving thing I have ever witnessed in sports. Knowing Johnny and being a part of the team when that happened was just unbelievable.

But you know, that most incredible moment has passed and is only a memory. Johnny Bench doesn't play baseball anymore, and one day I won't. What you have to base your life on must be something that *will* last. I only know of one thing that will do that, and now I only wish I had gotten to know Him sooner.

MITCH WEBSTER
Montreal Expos/Outfielder

"I Threw My Helmet And Had A Few Choice Words For The Umpire"

I used to have a terrible temper. It was nothing for me to throw my helmet, tell the umpire off, and punch somebody out in the same game. I look back now on those times when I thought I was being a macho man, and I realize I was really showing immaturity and lack of control.

I grew up in a very small town in Kansas. My dad played in the minor leagues in the San Francisco Giants organization, and he has been a coach for more than twenty-five years now. I had two older brothers who were outstanding athletes, and both played college ball. My high school didn't even have a baseball team, so I played basketball and ran track. I picked up baseball by playing with my brothers and by joining in games during the summer.

I was drafted after graduation from Larned High School in 1977 by the Toronto Blue Jays. There were many times when I wanted to quit, especially after spending seven years in the minors. But my

wife, Jennifer, and my friends kept encouraging me to stay with it.

I started the 1985 season in the majors with the Blue Jays, and it looked as though things were turning around. Then after 4 games and 1 at bat, I became a victim of the numbers game and was sent down to Syracuse. It just so happened that two other players on the Blue Jays had to be kept on the major-league roster or be returned to their former teams according to the rules of the draft in which they were obtained. So it was back to the minors for me.

If it hadn't been for my faith that the Lord was in control, I think I would have gone crazy. I was in junior high school when I accepted Christ, but I really didn't commit myself to Him until later on. I had a strong desire for consistency and self-control in my life, and I saw it only in other Christians. It was during this time in the minors that I realized I had to get into the Bible, and then I would start growing. So I did this through Bible studies with my teammates, and I've slowly developed some of that consistency and self-control I had always wanted.

I played 46 games for Syracuse and then was traded to the Expos in June 1985. I finished out the year in the majors, and it looks as though I'm going to be around for a while. I've been playing center field regularly since June 27, 1985, and finished that year batting .274. I got my first major-league home run on June 30 against Jerry Koosman and the Philadelphia Phillies. Then I homered twice against the Houston Astros and Bob Knepper in the Astrodome on July 4. Next I broke a long-standing club record from September 6–10 by homering in 4 consecutive games.

This past off-season, Jennifer and I joined the First Baptist Church in Great Bend, Kansas, and started their Survival Kit discipleship training. Now that the season has started, we have continued to have our daily quiet time while continuing the Survival Kit training. That study has taught us a lot about spiritual growth, and we can really feel it.

You know, it's a real long shot to make it to the major leagues. You just have to know what God wants you to do and then do it. I know that sounds simple, but it's so true. Sure it takes hard work, dedication, and discipline, but without the Lord in your life, you'll never make it and be happy, too.

WAYNE TOLLESON
New York Yankees/Infielder

"Bobby Richardson Was More Than A Great Baseball Player"

When I was in junior high school, I got to hear Bobby Richardson, an All-Star second baseman with the Yankees, speak at a banquet. After hearing him speak, my respect for him increased even more because of his commitment to Christ and the fact that his baseball career was built around that. That night really had an impact on my life.

While growing up in Spartanburg, South Carolina, I pretty much stayed out of trouble. I can see it was to my advantage to be brought up in a Christian home. And in our home, Dad was a strict disciplinarian who didn't spare the leather to my behind. Fortunately, he loved me enough to discipline me in whichever way was the most effective, and I'm very grateful. I can remember my parents taking me and my brother and sister to church only on Sunday mornings until we got older and they saw the need to be more involved in church. It is really great to look back and see as much spiritual growth in their lives as in mine.

After I graduated from Spartanburg High School in 1974, I was asked to sign with the New York Mets as a free agent. However, I really enjoyed playing football and basketball as well as baseball in high school, so I decided I wanted to play football and baseball in college. I turned down the Mets' offer. I wanted to go to the University of South Carolina and play for Bobby Richardson, who was the baseball coach there, but the university wouldn't let me play football, too. So I went to Western Carolina University, where I was able to play both sports. As a senior I was named an All-American as a wide receiver and led the NCAA in pass receptions. After graduation from Western Carolina, I felt I was ready to play pro baseball and was drafted by the Texas Rangers in the eighth round in 1978.

I finally made it to the major leagues for good in 1982. In 1983 I had a decent year, and then the bottom fell out in '84. My batting average dropped to .213, and I knew why. I was not doing anything drastically wrong like messing around with drugs, but I was not keeping my relationship up with the Lord. I had grown lazy in my Bible study and prayer time. That experience taught me a lot about being in close touch with the Lord on a daily basis. God dealt with me in an area where He could get my attention, baseball. In 1985 my wife, Kim, and I started the season right by attending the Professional Athletes Outreach Conference with other players and their wives. There we learned how to renew our commitment and grow as a family in our walk with Christ. It's no wonder my batting average in 1985 increased 100 points to .313! I believed Romans 8:28 before 1984, and I believe it even more now.

I think kids who really want to succeed in anything need to strive for consistency and commitment. In your faith you do this by communing with God on a daily basis. This will enable you to be the best athlete you can be. You see too many guys on the field who are too high and then too low, and they just can't compete to the best of their ability because they are inconsistent. They dwell too much on their mistakes—and sometimes too much on their accomplishments—to ever be able to compete athletically to a high degree. I really strive to be on an even temperament whether I go 0 for 4 or 4 for 4.

I got traded to the Chicago White Sox in 1986, and I was a little surprised after having such a good year with the Rangers. Then about halfway through the season I was traded to the Yankees. Well, that's baseball.

Now I'm with the team that my favorite baseball player, Bobby Richardson, spent his whole career with. I know God has a purpose in this, and I'm going to make the best of it! Without a doubt I know God is in control and has me right where He wants me. It sure is great to know that wherever you are, if you're in God's will, you're exactly where you are supposed to be.

TIM BURKE
Montreal Expos/Pitcher

"From The Minors To A Major-League Record In Eight Months"

Opening day, 1985, and there I was pitching against the Cincinnati Reds. I had been invited to spring training camp and had a pretty good spring. I had still been a long shot to make the team, but there I was, and I knew it was the Lord who put me there.

I grew up in Omaha, Nebraska, where I was real close to my family. My mom died while I was in high school, so I became even closer to my sister and my dad. Once I started playing baseball, I realized I was better than most kids my age and started driving myself to be the best. I graduated from Roncalli High School in 1977 and accepted a baseball scholarship to the University of Nebraska. I had always gone to church and usually did what I was supposed to do—until I got to college, that is.

At Nebraska I began to run around and do everything guys do in college. I started concentrating on baseball when I found out I was going to be a high draft pick. I attended Nebraska for three years and

made the All-Big-Eight team. When I was on the field, I worked hard on my baseball game. When I was off the field, I worked hard at having a good time. It was during this time that I developed a terrible drinking habit. The University of Nebraska is really known for its football team and all the parties they have every Saturday night after the home games. My alcohol habit got so bad that one season after four of six home games, I got so drunk that I couldn't find my car. I usually found my car the next day, but after one Saturday night it took me *six days* to find where I had left it. I tell you this not to brag, but to let you know the pathetic condition my life was in.

I was drafted in the second round in 1981 by the Pittsburgh Pirates and went off into pro baseball.

Then baseball became a business instead of a game. I knew that they were signing my paycheck and that if I didn't produce I would be gone. I didn't have a very good year, and to make problems worse, I turned to drinking alcohol even more. I thought getting married would help solve some of my problems, so at the beginning of my second year in the minors I got married. After two weeks of marriage, my wife Christine was all packed and ready to go home because I was a very selfish person. Some of my teammates got us to go to a Bible study, and it was there that I realized I was headed for destruction. I finally understood for the first time in my life that I needed to give my life to Christ. After learning the meaning of 1 Peter 5:7, I gave my life and all its problems to Jesus Christ to let Him handle them. Christine came to the same conclusion, and we started a new life together in August 1982.

Just because I became a Christian doesn't mean all my problems disappeared, but it does mean I now have a way of solving them. As long as I keep Him first in my life, I know everything will work out for my good. Now I just do the very best I can and leave the results up to Him, whatever they may be.

In 1983 I was traded to the New York Yankees organization, and I had a 12—4 record in 20 starts at Nashville in AA ball. At the end of that season, I was dealt to the Expos, who sent me to Indianapolis in AAA ball. One year later, in 1985, I finally made it to the big leagues. On the final day of the season, I tied the major-league record for appearances in a game by a rookie pitcher (78) set by Ed Vande Berg of the Seattle Mariners in 1982. That total was also good enough to lead the National League. I had shutout streaks of 10 innings, 13 innings, and 24 innings. During one three-month period, I was 5–0 with 4 saves and a 0.70 ERA. Also in that stretch, I allowed only 5 earned runs in 51⅔ innings. It was a pretty exciting year!

Every once in a while I start worrying about my wins and losses and my ERA going up. Then the Lord gently reminds me that I am trying to handle myself again, after I gave my life to Him to handle. You know, I could blow my arm out tomorrow and never play again. If that happened, I know it would be difficult to deal with. But then I realize God has not made a mistake yet, and He never will, because He knows what's best for me.

JOE JOHNSON
Toronto Blue Jays/Pitcher

"From AA Ball To The Big Leagues In One Year"

Playing baseball has been my life as far back as I can remember. Even when I was in high school, my parents could see that I might have a shot at being a professional baseball player, so they told me to play ball and they would provide me with a car and spending money so I could concentrate on my game.

I graduated from King Phillip Regional High School in Wrentham, Massachusetts, in 1979. Right away I had to make a big decision. I was drafted by the Phillies, but my parents really wanted me to have a college education. My dad told the Phillies that I would sign if they would give me a bonus equal to four years of college education. They said no, so I didn't sign. Looking back now, I sure am grateful for my father's wisdom in that situation. A few weeks later I got a scholarship offer from the University of Maine, and off I went.

I really enjoyed college baseball and was privileged to go to two College World Series in Omaha,

Nebraska. My senior year I won 2 games in the Series and beat the number-one-rated team, Cal-State, Fullerton, by pitching a 4-hit shutout. That game just happened to be the day before the draft, and my worth went up considerably. The Atlanta Braves drafted me in the second round of that 1982 draft and sent me to their Savannah farm club.

I really had dreams of making it big in baseball, so I built my whole life around it. Then in my third year of pro ball, the game failed me! I was playing AAA ball in Richmond, Virginia, and lost 2 straight games. They sent me back down to their AA team in Savannah, where I promptly lost 5 games in a row. I was 0–7 and really had no hope of getting better. I had already started thinking about going home a failure and deciding what kind of job I would look for.

There were two different groups of guys on that Savannah team. First there were the guys who wanted to party and constantly look for the good times. Then there were three guys who were Christians and really had something to hold on to even if they had to quit baseball. That's what I wanted, because the other guys had nothing that would last. I started going to Bible studies with these guys and began to understand just what they had. One morning while on a road trip in Columbus, Georgia, I was watching a television preacher named Jimmy Swaggart, and God really spoke to me. I got down on my knees in that hotel room and asked Jesus into my heart.

What happened after that I call a miracle. I gained a new confidence I never thought existed. I knew I was where God wanted me to be, and I finished out the season in pretty good shape.

The next year I was sent to Greenville, South Carolina, where I pitched well and then was sent up to AAA ball in Richmond again. I was later called up to the big leagues in Atlanta, where I finished out the season. From AA ball to the majors in one season. Wow! That's incredible!

I got married last year to a great Christian girl. We make our home in Plainville, Massachusetts. When we are in Atlanta, we attend First Baptist Church, where we get great teaching from Dr. Charles Stanley in a live, Spirit-filled church.

About halfway through the season I was traded to the Blue Jays for Doyle Alexander. I finished the season there in a divisional race where we came up short. But we'll be back.

Kids who think they want to be big-league ballplayers have to really love the game. To be the best ballplayer you can possibly be, you also have to make a decision. Are you going to follow the crowd that leads to nowhere and will not last, or will you make the decision to do what is right and will last more than a lifetime?

Steps to a Personal Relationship With God

Each of these players has spoken of a personal relationship with Jesus Christ. If you desire to have this personal relationship, just do the following:

Believe:
- God loves you and has a specific purpose for your life.
- Sin (disobedience of God) keeps you from knowing Him.
- Jesus Christ died on the cross for your sins so you can know Him personally.
- You must invite Jesus Christ to come into your life and take control.

Pray:
Just simply bow your head and talk to Jesus Christ repeating and believing this simple prayer: Lord Jesus, I believe you made full payment for my sin when you died on the cross. I ask you to forgive me of my sin, come into my life, and take total control of my life.

If you prayed this prayer, the Bible, God's Word, says that Jesus Christ is now in your heart. Please write us at the following address, and we will be very happy to send you more information about your new personal relationship with Jesus Christ.

Hillwood Ministries
6 Rutland Road
Mt. Juliet, TN 37122

Sportspower Ministries

Sportspower Ministries was founded in 1980 to manifest the power of Jesus Christ through the world of sports. Founder Bill Alexson, through the encouragement of one of the founders of NFL chapels, pioneered the chapel program for the National Basketball Association. He now works with other ministries in counseling and teaching the pros, through Bible studies and conferences, how they can have new life and purpose beyond professional sports. He was also a contributor to Batting a Thousand and is co-author of Reaching for the Rim.

Sportspower Ministries has sent more than two hundred pros into two hundred schools in eight states to share their lives and commitment to Jesus Christ.

If you would like more information about Sportspower Ministries, write to:

Bill Alexson
Sportspower Ministries
P.O. Box 433
Lee, MA 01238

For Information about other Christian Sports
Ministries, Contact the Following:

Fellowship of Christian Athletes
8701 Leeds Road
Kansas City, Missouri 64129

Athletes in Action
6264 Lehman Drive
Suite A-101
Colorado Springs, Colorado 80918

Professional Athletes Outreach
P.O. Box 1044
Issaqua, Washington 98027

Institute For Athletic Perfection
P.O. Box 627
Branson, Missouri 65616

About the Author

Terry Hill is a graduate of Bryan College and a noted Christian journalist and marketing executive. He lives with his wife, Dianne, and their four children in Mount Juliet, Tennessee.